Shapes: Triangles

Esther Sarfatti

Rourke
Publishing LLC
Vero Beach, Florida 32964

www.rourkepublishing.com

PHOTO CREDITS: © Marilyn Nieves: title page; © Stas Volik: page 5; © Nicholas Monu: page 7; © Stephen Walls: page 9; © Kenneth C. Zirkel: page 11; © Christine Balderas: page 13; © Viktor Kitaykin: page 15; © Joan Kimball: page 17; © Tristin Hurst: page 23.

Editor: Robert Stengard-Olliges

Cover design by Nicola Stratford.

Library of Congress Cataloging-in-Publication Data

Sarfatti, Esther.
  Shapes : triangles / Esther Sarfatti.
    p. cm. -- (Concepts)
  ISBN 978-1-60044-528-6 (Hardcover)
  ISBN 978-1-60044-669-6 (Softcover)
  1. Triangle--Juvenile literature. 2. Shapes--Juvenile literature. I. Title.
  QA482.S36 2008
  516'.154--dc22
                                    2007014076

Printed in the USA

CG/CG

Rourke Publishing

www.rourkepublishing.com – rourke@rourkepublishing.com
Post Office Box 3328, Vero Beach, FL 32964

This is a triangle.

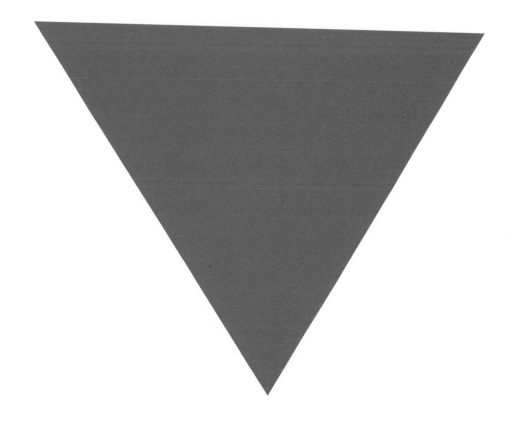

Triangles are everywhere.

This roof has a triangle.

These sandwiches are triangles.

These windows are triangles.

This ice cream cone is
a triangle.

Some guitars are triangles.

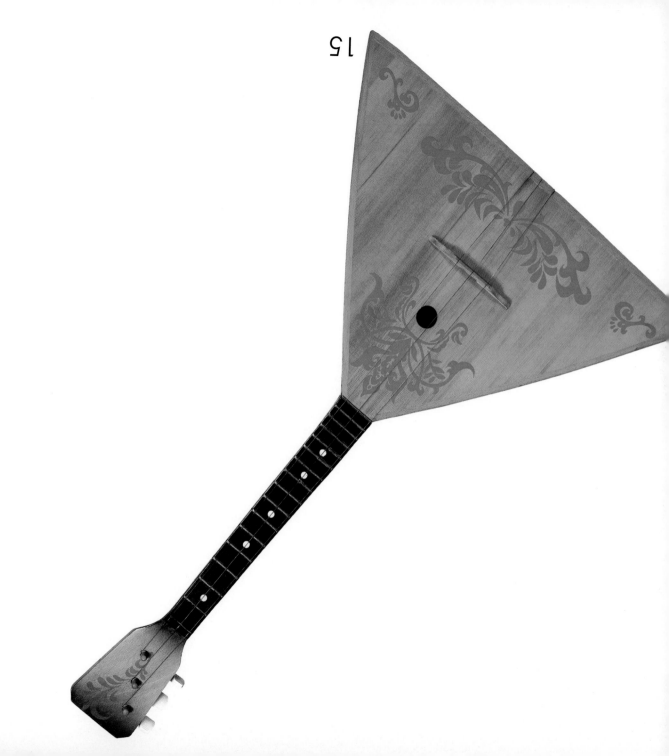

This quilt has triangles.

This piece of pie is
a triangle.

This cheese is a triangle.

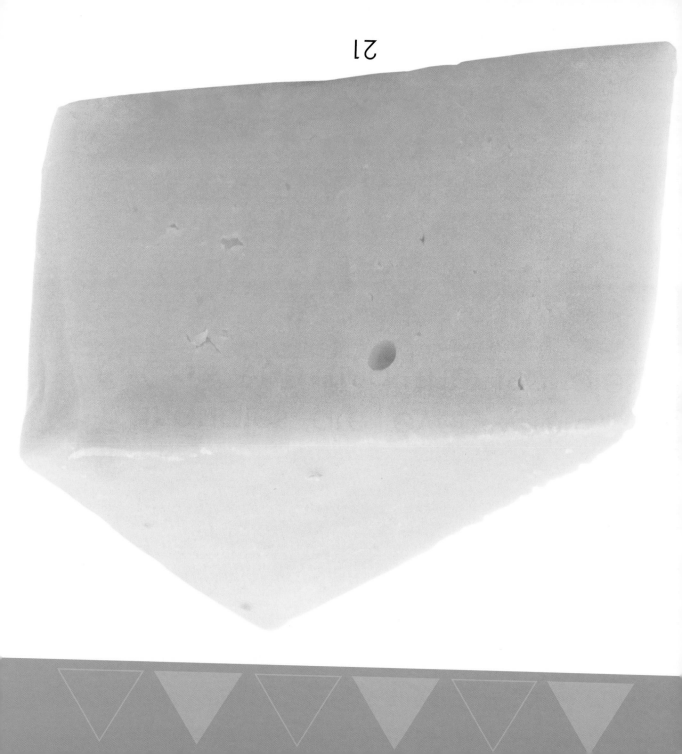

Triangles are everywhere.
Can you find the triangles?

Index

Further Reading

Leake, Diyan. *Finding Shapes: Triangles*. Heinemann, 2005.
Olson, Nathan. *Triangles Around Town*. A+ Books, 2007.

Recommended Websites
www.enchantedlearning.com/themes/shapes.shtml

About the Author
Esther Sarfatti has worked with children's books for over 15 years as an editor and translator. This is her first series as an author. Born in Brooklyn, New York, and brought up in a trilingual home, Esther currently lives with her husband and son in Madrid, Spain.